SCAREDY CATS

written and illustrated by Audrey Wood

Child's Play (International) Ltd

Swindon   Auburn ME   Sydney

© MCMLXXX M. Twinn   This edition 2005
ISBN 1-904550-48-7   Printed in Croatia
        1 3 5 7 9 10 8 6 4 2
www.childs-play.com

One busy morning, Mother Cat sat down and wrote
a letter. When she finished, she had a problem.

Mother Cat called her seven children. Which two would go to town and mail the letter?

Everyone wanted to go. Finally, Mother Cat chose her two eldest kittens.

Her youngest kittens were very sad.
They had never been to town without Mother Cat.
Why couldn't they have a chance?

How the older kittens laughed! Send the babies to town? Even shadows scared them. They would never make it.

But Mother Cat was fair. She knew the little kittens were right. It was their turn, after all.

Mother Cat gave
the letter to her
youngest yellow kitten,
and a coin to her
youngest blue kitten.

Proud and puffed-up,
the happy kittens
started on their way
to town.

The road ahead seemed
to go on and on forever.

Each step took the kittens farther
and farther away from home.

Suddenly, Yellow Kitten began to wonder
and worry about scarey things.
"What if something bad happens?
What if you lose Mother's coin?"

"What if I sneeze," Blue Kitten agreed,
"and the coin jumps out of my paw?"

"And it starts rolling away," Yellow Kitten added,
"faster and faster and faster?"

"And then it hides,"
Blue Kitten said,
"and we cannot find it?"

But the scaredy cats
did not turn back.
They walked on
down the road to town.

Before long, the kittens came to the bridge.
Suddenly, Blue Kitten began to wonder and worry
about scarey things. "What if something awful happens
when we cross over?
What if someone steals Mother's coin?"

"What if a giant troll cat jumps up out of the water,"
Yellow Kitten agreed, "growling and yowling at us?"
"And he grabs us and shakes us," Blue Kitten added,
"and wants to eat us up?"

"And he sees the coin shining in our paws," Yellow Kitten said, "and takes it from us?"

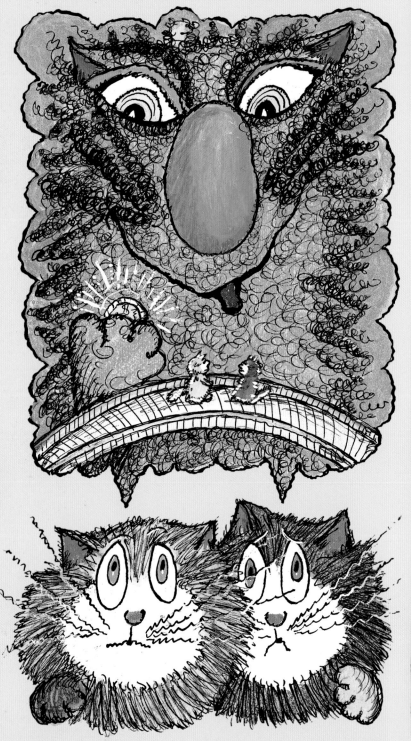

The scaredy cats thought about turning back, but they kept on going.

On the other side of the bridge, the kittens
tiptoed into the forest. Suddenly, Yellow Kitten
began to wonder and worry about scarey things.
"What if something dreadful happens?
What if I lose Mother's letter?"

"What if a howling wind comes along?"
Blue Kitten agreed, "and rips the letter
out of your paws?"
"And the wind throws the letter down
into the leaves?" Yellow Kitten added.

"And we look and look for it, until we are grey and whiskered," Blue Kitten said, "but never find it?" Even though the scaredy cats wanted to go back home, they kept on walking through the forest.

Soon, they came to the long, dark tunnel.
Suddenly, Blue Kitten began to wonder
and worry about scarey things.
"What if something terrible happens?
What if someone steals Mother's letter?"

"What if cat-bandits are inside, waiting for us?"
Yellow Kitten agreed.

"What if they have claws like knives," Blue Kitten
added, "and red-gleaming cat eyes?"

"And they surround us,"
Yellow Kitten said,
"and tie us up with ropes,
and leave us shivering
in the dark, cold tunnel?"

Still, the scaredy cats
kept on going, through
the tunnel and out
the other side.

There, they found the nettle field. The kittens walked
on through the tall weeds. Suddenly, Yellow Kitten
began to wonder and worry about scarey things.
"What if something woeful happens? What if we get lost?"

"What if an evil cat-witch casts a spell,"
Blue Kitten agreed, "and turns the whole
world into nettle fields?"
"And all the cats and towns are lost and
hidden in the nettles," Yellow Kitten added,
"and we never find the Post Office?"

The scaredy cats wished they could go back home, but they walked on through the nettles, until they came to the high, rocky ledge.

Suddenly, Blue Kitten began to wonder and worry about scarey things. "What if something hideous happens? What if someone steals us?"

"What if a great, screeching bird snatches us?"
Yellow Kitten agreed.
"And takes us to its nest, high on a mountain top,"
Blue Kitten added.

"And," Yellow Kitten said, "we have to feed
and care for its ugly babies."

Even now,
the scaredy cats
kept on going.
They did not turn back.

Hurray! At the bottom
of the ledge, the kittens
came into town,
and the Post Office
was not hard to find.

But when they ran up to the door, a truly bad and awful and dreadful and terrible and woeful and hideous thing happened. The Post Office was closed for the day. Now, Mother's coin could not buy a stamp. Mother's letter could not be mailed. How could the kittens go home without finishing their job?

Just then, the kittens had a wonderful surprise.
A bus drove up and Grandmother Cat stepped out.
No one knew she was coming to Catville.

The kittens told her about Mother's very important letter, and about the scarey things.

When Grandmother Cat looked at the letter, it was her turn to be surprised. The letter was for her! She opened it, and read out loud.

Before they left Catville,
Grandmother Cat
took the kittens to the
ice cream parlour.
She treated them all
to fishberry cones.

Which way are the bandits? Show me that old Troll Cat. You say there's a witch up ahead?

Follow us Grandmother!

We know the way!

At last, the kittens started for home,
with Grandmother Cat following close behind.
On the way, they wondered and worried
about scarey things – but not very much.

The End